DONNA BERGMAN

Timmy Green's Blue Lake

ILLUSTRATED BY IB OHLSSON

TAMBOURINE BOOKS  NEW YORK

Library of Congress Cataloging in Publication Data
Bergman, Donna   Timmy Green's blue lake/by Donna Bergman; illustrated by Ib Ohlsson—1st ed.   p.   cm.
Summary: Timmy Green, who loves anything blue, uses his imagination
to turn an old sheet of blue plastic into a lake, road, and space shuttle.
ISBN 0-688-10747-8.—ISBN 0-688-10748-6 (lib. bdg.)
[1. Imagination—Fiction.   2. Blue—Fiction.]   I. Ohlsson, Ib., 1935- ill.   II. Title.   PZ7.B45222Ti   1992
[E]—dc20
91-30232   CIP   AC

1   3   5   7   9   10   8   6   4   2
First Edition

For Doug
D. B.

For Ria
I. O.

Timmy Green loved anything blue: his bicycle and football helmet, blueberry pie and the blue of the sky, his old blue T-shirt, and, most of all, his blue marble collection.

One summer day, when Barney Baxter, Chucky Sullivan, and even Sherry Lou Sweet, the girl next door, were away on vacation, Timmy went outside to play.

He found some blue plastic that had once covered the woodpile. He grabbed it and shook it out. The plastic made a crackling sound.

Timmy spread the blue cover out on the grass. The sun warmed and softened the plastic. It seemed to ripple and flow. Timmy studied it. "This is the famous Blue Lake," he proclaimed. "It can be terribly treacherous."

Timmy parked his wagon on the lakeshore nearest the woodpile. "This is the city of Slurpy Shores."

Then he rode his bike around the lake and parked it on the opposite shore. "This is the city of Wheelyville."

Next he put on a painter's cap and life jacket. Fully uniformed
and ready to sail, he stepped onto his skateboard.

As ship's captain, he sailed The Blue Whale back and forth
across Blue Lake carrying treasures from port to port.

Midway through his third crossing seabirds swooped and soared overhead. And they screamed, which is what they always did before a storm. The captain strained to listen for distant thunder.

With the first clap, the sun disappeared and the wind kicked up and the sea began to swell. The captain struggled to keep a tight hold on the wheel. He held on until the storm blew itself out.

Late in the day the sun reappeared and he brought the ship safely into port. The tired captain went directly to his sleeping quarters.

The next morning the weather was cloudy and cold. The captain shivered as he bent down to test Blue Lake's water. It felt stiff and hard.

Timmy bolted up when someone shouted, "Hi, Timmy. Guess what? I'm back."

It was Sherry Lou Sweet. Seconds later she stood next to Timmy on the shores of Blue Lake.

"What's that terrible-looking blue thing?" she asked.

"Blue Lake," Timmy said.

"It can't be a lake. Doesn't look a bit like water."

"Well, it is," Timmy said. "It's just that…due to the weather…Blue Lake is frozen."

"Then let's go skating," Sherry Lou said.

"Oh, I don't think that's a good idea," Timmy said, but Sherry Lou ran to get her skates anyway. Soon she teetered on the ice. Her ankles wobbled as she fought to keep her balance. Slowly, she slid one foot in front of another.

"I didn't fall once," she said when back on land.

"Very good," Timmy replied, but then he looked closely at his lake. Her skates had sliced it into three strips.

"Look!" Timmy shouted. "You should never, never have gone skating."

"Guess that's the end of Blue Lake," Sherry Lou said.

That afternoon the weather improved and Timmy took the
three blue strips and laid them end to end. "This is a fine road,"
he said.

The road began at the woodpile. It ended at the doghouse, where Timmy's dog, Sam, sprawled.

As an officer of the law, Timmy hopped on his motorcycle and roared up and down the road checking on speeders.

By lunchtime, when Officer Tim pulled his motorcycle into the garage, he had issued eight speeding tickets, eleven warnings, and hauled two people to the police station.

    Before long Sherry Lou returned. She pointed to the road.
"What's that?"
    "A road," Timmy answered.
    "Roads aren't blue."
    "Mine is."
    "Well, if it *is* a road," she said, "there should be some place
along it where thirsty drivers and policemen can get a drink
—like lemonade."

Timmy was thirsty. So they built a stand and mixed lemonade.
That afternoon Sherry Lou sold five glasses.

After dinner Sherry Lou dressed in her mother's clothes and turned up in Timmy's yard. She wore black high-heeled shoes with sparkling buckles.

"It's such a nice evening. Let's walk along your road," she said.

"I need to fix my motorcycle," Timmy replied.

"You can fix it later. We can walk first," Sherry Lou said.

"Oh, all right," Timmy said.

They walked all the way to Sam's doghouse and back. "My feet hurt," Sherry Lou complained.

Timmy looked down at her shoes. Just then he noticed that her high heels had punched hundreds of holes in his road. Blades of grass stuck up through the holes. Now his blue road had green polka dots.

"Honestly, Sherry Lou, just look at what you've done this time. As of this very minute, my road is closed to all high heels. In fact, it's completely closed for repairs."

The next morning Timmy went out to look at his road. But Sam had a chunk of it clenched between his teeth. Playfully he ran back and forth and growled. "Sam!" Timmy shouted, "put my road down." Sam dropped it.

The other two sections of road were wadded up in front of Sam's doghouse. The road was beyond repair.

Timmy collected the shreds and folded them neatly.
Suddenly, he dashed into the house where he built the frame-
work for a tiny kite.

When the frame was done Timmy stretched a scrap of blue plastic over it. For a tail he tacked on streamers cut from another piece. Finally he attached a long spool of thread to the kite.

He called Sherry Lou over for the launch. The blue kite sailed up. It looped and soared. Its tail fluttered.

Up still higher it went, until Timmy could no longer see it and until all the thread was let out. Then he did what he'd planned to do all along. He let the thread go.

"You shouldn't have done that," Sherry Lou said. "You'll never see it again."

"Yes I will. My space ship is on a mission—orbiting the world," Timmy said. "I expect it to land back here a year from now."